Pet Sitter

BEWARE THE WEREPUP

JULIE SYKES

ILLUSTRATED BY
NATHAN REED

KINGFISHER
NEW YORK

For Daniel and Jamie—J. S.
For Joseph—N. R.

KINGFISHER
LONDON & NEW YORK

Text copyright © 2009 by Julie Sykes
Illustrations copyright © 2009 by Nathan Reed
Published in the United States by Kingfisher,
175 Fifth Ave., New York, NY 10010
Kingfisher is an imprint of Macmillan Children's Books, London.

Distributed in the U.S. by Macmillan, 175 Fifth Ave., New York, NY 10010
Distributed in Canada by H.B. Fenn and Company Ltd., 34 Nixon Road,
Bolton, Ontario L7E 1W2

Library of Congress Cataloging-in-Publication data has been applied for.

ISBN: 978-0-7534-6218-8

Kingfisher books are available for special promotions and premiums. For details contact:
Special Markets Department, Macmillan, 175 Fifth Avenue, New York, NY 10010.

For more information, please visit www.kingfisherpublications.com

First American Edition September 2009
Printed and bound in the U.K. by CPI Mackays, Chatham ME5 8TD
1 3 5 7 9 8 6 4 2

CONTENTS

Chapter One
Seagull Towers

The phone was ringing. Max dashed out of his bedroom, raced down the stairs, and snatched it up.

"Hello," he said. "This is Max the Pet Sitter."

"Hello, Max," said a cheery voice. "This is Ned Nettles the Pet Owner. Can you pet sit for me? I'm going away for a week to help out my sister. She runs a children's camp, and one of her employees is sick."

"Sure," said Max. "What sort of pet do you have?"

"A puppy," said Ned. "He's adorable.

Why not come over to meet him? I live at Apartment Six, Seagull Towers."

"I'm on my way," said Max, and he put down the phone.

Max wrote Ned's address in his pet-sitter notebook and then hurried out to the yard to get his bike from the shed. Mom was weeding the rose bed.

"Going somewhere?" she asked, waving a trowel at him.

"Seagull Towers, to meet a puppy and a man named Ned Nettles."

"That'll be fun," said Mom. "You've always wanted a puppy."

It was true. Max desperately wanted a pet of his own, but he couldn't have one because his annoying big sister, Alice, was allergic to animals. As Max rode to Seagull Towers, he wondered what the puppy would be like. Ned Nettles had called his pet adorable, and Max imagined a cute little animal with floppy ears and big brown eyes. Ned sounded nice, too. Max decided he would be young and friendly with a smiley face.

It wasn't far to Seagull Towers. Max pedaled up the driveway and stopped in surprise next to a large sign.

"'Seagull Towers,'" he read. "'No Skateboards. No Ball Games. No Pets. By Order of the Caretaker.'"

That couldn't be right! Max pulled his pet-sitter notebook out of his pocket to check that he had the right address.

He was flipping through the pages when a voice called out, "Hello, are you Max?"

Max looked up. Seagull Towers was a huge old house with three floors and two turrets. A very grand stone staircase led up to an enormous revolving front door, and standing at the top of it was a wrinkled old man with spiky silver hair.

"Max?" he called again, and when Max nodded, the man swung a leg over the stone handrail and slid down the banister.

"Ned Nettles," he said, almost landing on Max's toes. "Thanks for coming so quickly."

"All part of the service," said Max, trying not to laugh.

Since taking his first pet-sitting job, Max had met all sorts of unusual pets and their owners, and Ned was no exception! There was green glitter in his spiky silver hair and he wore star-shaped green and silver glasses. Pinned to his black shirt was a lifelike spider badge. He wasn't at all like what Max had imagined.

"Park your bike there. Then you can meet Fang," said Ned.

Max pointed at the sign. "But I thought—"

"Thinking can be dangerous," Ned interrupted. "Hurry up."

As Max chained his bike to the signpost, something hit him in the back of the legs.

"Oomph!" he spluttered, almost head butting his back wheel. He spun around.

"Woo, woo, wooooo!" panted a messy bundle of gray fur. "Woo, woo, wooooo!"

"Nice dog," said Max, hesitantly putting out a hand and then pulling it back again when he saw the size of the dog's teeth.

"Quiet, Fang," hissed Ned, and then, "Fang, that's naughty."

Fang was attacking the signpost. Ned pulled him away and then prized a long splinter of wood from the puppy's mouth.

"How many times have I told you not to chew?" he said, pretending to be angry.

Max gasped. Fang's teeth must have been really sharp to do that amount of damage. He hoped the puppy was going to be friendly. It would have been awful if Fang decided to take a chunk out of him!

"Fang, say hello to Max."

Ned let the puppy go again.

"Woooooo, woo, woo, wooooo!" squealed Fang, rushing back to Max.

Fang had wolflike blue eyes, a long snout, and wicked claws. Max tensed as Fang jumped toward him, but the puppy just wanted to lick him. Max laughed, patting the parts of the leaping Fang he could reach, until he realized he was standing in a puddle.

"Whoops! Someone's had an accident." Max lifted a sodden sneaker.

"That's no accident." Ned grinned. "It's a compliment. Fang's excited. He does that when he really likes someone."

"Nice!" said Max. "So what does he do to people he doesn't like?"

Ned tapped the side of his nose. "Best not ask," he said.

CHAPTER TWO
A SECRET

"Come see my apartment," said Ned once Fang had calmed down.

Ned hurried up the stone staircase, and Max had to run to catch up with him as he disappeared through the revolving door. Max followed, and the door whisked him around and spat him out so quickly that he landed on his bottom in the lobby. A large woman with a chin as bristly as a porcupine peered over the counter.

"Morning, Ned, and who's that?"

Ned hauled Max to his feet.

"This is Max the Plant Sitter. He's going

to water my plants for me while I'm away.
Max, meet Bertha Crab, our caretaker."

Max opened his mouth to correct Ned
and then shut it again in surprise as Ned
slyly kicked his ankle. He looked around
for Fang, but the puppy seemed to have
disappeared.

"Hello, Bertha," said Max.

"It's Mrs. Crab to you," sniffed the

caretaker, glaring at Max. "I hope you're going to behave yourself. The rules are clearly—"

"Yes, yes," interrupted Ned impatiently. "Thank you, Bertha, but we've got to dash. Come along, Max."

Ned's apartment was in one of the turrets. He led the way up a spiral staircase to a hallway on the second floor and stopped at a door numbered six.

"Here we are."

Deftly, Ned unpinned his spider badge and threw it at the door. A long silver thread, attached to a tiny cobweb on Ned's shirt, followed the spider. When it hit the door, the spider scuttled up to the lock, stuck one leg inside the keyhole, and wiggled it. The door opened.

Max gawped and then jumped as Fang appeared suddenly by his feet.

"Where did you go?" he asked as the puppy barged past him.

"Fang is very good at being invisible," Ned said, chuckling. He stuck the spider back on his shirt. "In you go, Max."

Max stepped inside Ned's apartment, peeping curiously into the rooms as Ned led the way to the kitchen. In the living room, stars dangled from the ceiling, and in the bedroom, there was everything from a cauldron to a pointed green hat.

"Why did you tell Mrs. Crab that I'm a plant sitter?" he asked.

"Haven't you figured it out yet?" Ned stopped and shook his head. "And I thought you were smart!"

"You said that thinking can be dangerous," Max reminded him.

Ned roared with laughter. "True, but I need some excitement, living here. There are far too many silly rules. No skateboards, no ball games, NO PETS. No fun, if you ask me."

"Sounds about as interesting as watching a cauldron rust," Max agreed.

"It was!" said Ned. "Until I found Fang. Someone left him on the beach, tied up in a sack, with the tide coming in. How could they? Fang's the most adorable werepup in the world."

"A werepup?!" exclaimed Max. "Wicked."

"Wicked he is, too," Ned agreed. "Spider's teeth, Fang has livened things up! I've had to keep Fang a secret because of the silly no-pets rule, but I've had him for more than a week, and no one's guessed yet! Not even nosy old Bertha Crab."

"So, if anyone asks, I'm here to look after your plants."

"That's right," said Ned, perching against the kitchen table. "You mustn't tell anyone about Fang."

"How do I take him out for walks?" asked Max.

Ned opened a cabinet and brought out an enormous wicker basket with a frilly red cover.

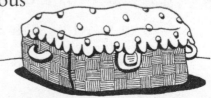

"You'll have to

smuggle him out of the building in this," he announced.

Max eyed the basket suspiciously.

"No way! I'll look like Little Red Riding Hood!" he protested.

Ned's cheerful face turned serious.

"Bertha Crab, the caretaker, is even crabbier than her name suggests. If she finds out about Fang, she'll make him leave, or worse. Bertha used to have a dog, until it chewed her favorite slippers. She was so mad that she said the dog was dangerous and made the vet put it to sleep."

"That's evil!" exclaimed Max.

"I know." Ned gripped Max's arm. "That's why you have to promise to keep Fang a secret."

"I promise," said Max solemnly. "I'm good at keeping secrets. I get tons of practice with my sister, Alice."

"Good," said Ned. "You'll have to be very careful. Bertha Crab is a pain. She's never around when you need her, yet she's sure to show up like a bad rash when you don't. And there's one more thing: remember, Fang is a werepup. Never take him out at night. NEVER! There's a full moon soon, and anything could happen! Got that? Okay, I'll show you what he eats. You'll also need a key and your pay."

CHAPTER THREE
HOWLING IN THE NIGHT

Max couldn't wait to start pet sitting Fang. He loved animals, and he loved a challenge, but the first challenge came quicker than he thought. When Max arrived at Seagull Towers the following morning, Mrs. Crab was waiting for him.

"There was an awful racket last night," she said, glaring at him over the counter in the lobby. "It was coming from Ned's apartment, and it sounded like an animal."

Max's stomach turned a somersault. The noise had to be Fang, but why? Max hoped he wasn't hurt.

Mrs. Crab stood up.

"I think I'd better come with you to investigate."

Max did some quick thinking.

"Sorry, Mrs. Crab," he apologized. "Ned must have left the radio on. He loves listening to music."

"Music!" exclaimed Mrs. Crab. "That was music? It sounded like an animal in pain."

"It was probably opera." Max fumbled in his pocket for Ned's spare key. "That's painful to listen to."

Quickly, Max climbed the spiral staircase and then hurried down the hallway. It was very quiet. Too quiet. Max felt slightly sick and wasn't sure whether it was because of the winding staircase or worry. Something fluttered in his hand as he pulled out the spare spider badge that Ned had given him. He opened his palm, jumping as the spider leaped for the door.

"What was that?"

Max spun around. Mrs. Crab had followed him upstairs.

"Nothing," he said, raising his hand to the door and pretending to unlock it, even though the spider was doing the job quite nicely by itself.

"Bye, Mrs. Crab."

Max slid around the door and then

quickly shut it again. There was a squeak and a loud thud from the other side. Max lifted the mail slot and saw the caretaker squashed against the door like a bug on a car windshield. Silently chuckling to

himself, he headed for the kitchen to see what had upset Fang.

Max pushed open the kitchen door and gasped at the mess inside. The table lay upside down in the corner of the room. Two chairs were on top of the stove. The trash can was wedged inside the washing machine, and a mountain of food covered the floor. Perched seesawlike on the food mountain was a broken shelf.

"Fang," called Max. "Where are you?"

"Help!"

Max spun around. He'd expected Fang to

bark, not talk. Was someone playing a joke?

"Fang, is that you?"

"Well, it's not Ned," replied Fang smartly.

Max grinned. He'd taken care of talking animals before, but it was still a surprise to hear an animal speak for the first time. Max picked his way through the mess until he saw a black nose peeping out from beneath a box of Witchos.

"What happened?" he asked, pushing the Witchos aside. "Were you hungry?"

"Starving," agreed Fang, wiggling free.

 He threw himself at Max and licked his face. "Mmm, you taste good."

"Yuck!" Max pushed the puppy away. "Go lick something else."

Fang stopped licking Max's face and started on his shoes.

"What happened here?" asked Max.

"I don't know," said Fang sheepishly. "It was almost a full moon last night. I could see it through a chink in the curtain, and it made me want to howl. Then I got hungry and went to get a snack. Only, my biscuits are on the top shelf, and I couldn't reach them. I was nibbling one of Ned's sticks to take my mind off my rumbling belly when suddenly there was a bang and everything fell on top of me. I howled for help, but no one came."

"No one knows you're here," said Max. "Ned's keeping you a secret because of the no-pets rule. No more howling. If you get found out, you'll have to leave."

Fang's blue eyes grew as large as cauldrons.

"I don't want to leave. Ned's soooo nice!"

Max bent to pick up the chewed stick.

"Are you sure you're allowed to have this?"

"Yes," said Fang, licking Max's nose. "It's not Ned's best one. It's a spare. Mmm, you taste yummy."

"Get off!" Max laughed.

The stick looked familiar, but it was so

badly chewed that Max couldn't
figure out its function, so he
propped it up against
the washing machine.

"I'll clean up while
you eat breakfast. Then
we'll go out."

"Yippee!" squealed Fang.

Max slid off his backpack and dropped it
on the floor.

"I brought sandwiches, drinks, and a ball.
I thought we could go to the beach. I know
a nice one that's never crowded."

"Ooooh! Yes, yes, yes!" Fang ran around
in excited circles, almost knocking Max over.

"Calm down!" Max said, laughing.

Ned had left a huge supply of puppy
food. Max dished up a whole can of Meaty
Chunks, mixed it with a handful of dog

biscuits, and then refilled Fang's water bowl with fresh water. He cleaned up the kitchen while Fang ate.

"I'll put the broken shelf here," he said, placing it on a counter. "Please don't break anything else. Ned won't be happy if he comes back to a wrecked apartment."

Fang grunted. He was busy pushing his bowl around in circles on the floor as he licked it clean.

"Yummy." He sighed. "That was delicious."

The wicker basket he was supposed to use to smuggle Fang from the building was next to a blackened cauldron. Under the silly frilly cover Max found a collar, an extension leash, a small plastic shovel for scooping up poo, and a stack of plastic bags to put the poo in.

"Nice," he said, pushing it all toward one end to make room. "In you go."

The moment Fang dived into the basket, there was a loud crack. "Whoops!" yelped Fang. "Didn't see that there."

"Oops!" Max laughed, picking up the broken shovel. "Luckily for me, it's the handle end that broke."

Max pulled the cover back over the basket and pushed the stray tufts of Fang's gray fur out of sight.

"Ready?" he asked.

"Ready," was the muffled reply.

"Don't make a sound. I don't even want to hear you breathing," Max joked.

CHAPTER FOUR

WHERE IS MRS. CRAB?

Max needed both hands to lift the basket. He staggered a few paces and then dumped it on the floor.

"Oomph!" he groaned. "What a load!"

"Must be those Meaty Chunks," said Fang.

"It's *this* meaty chunk," teased Max, pulling back the cover and poking Fang's round belly. "You're too heavy for me to carry you in this. How does Ned manage?"

"Ned doesn't use the basket. He says a funny rhyme that makes me invisible," said Fang.

"Cool!" said Max. He'd guessed Ned was a wizard after seeing some of the things he kept in his apartment. That must be how he had gotten Fang out and then back inside the building yesterday when they'd first met. He'd said the puppy was good at being invisible. Max realized that Ned hadn't been joking.

"Well, I can't do magic, so I'll have to find another way of sneaking you outside."

Max thought for a moment and then had a brain wave.

"You can ride in my backpack. It's much lighter than the basket."

It was a squeeze to fit Fang inside the backpack. Max left the zipper partly open so Fang could breathe.

"Wheeee! This is FUN!" shouted Fang as Max hoisted the bag onto his back.

"Shh!" whispered Max. "We're leaving now."

Max opened the door to the apartment and headed cautiously for the stairs. He wished he'd remembered to tell Fang to stay still. Every now and then the puppy wiggled, which was a bit of a giveaway. But he shouldn't have worried. There was no sign of Mrs. Crab in the lobby, but there was a long line of people at the counter waiting to see her.

"She's never around when she's needed," grumbled one.

"I spend half my days looking for her," added another.

Nervously, Max looked around. Where had Mrs. Crab gone after she'd followed him up to Ned's apartment? Maybe she was hiding somewhere, waiting to catch him? She had to be up to something, or she would have been back in reception by then doing her job. Well, she wasn't going to catch Max. He was a good pet sitter. No way was he going to let Mrs. Crab find out about Fang. Ned had made it very clear what Mrs. Crab would do to Fang if she caught him. She'd make him leave, or worse.

"Mrs Crab is evil," Max muttered as he hurried to the door.

Safely outside, Max stood at the bottom of the stone steps while he decided on the quickest way to the beach.

"Pssst," whispered Fang. "You can let me out now."

32

Max waited until he was almost at the end of the driveway before he stopped. The backpack was heavy and he was glad to wiggle out of it and let Fang free. The moment Max unzipped his backpack, Fang leaped out and stretched his legs.

Suddenly a squirrel burst out from a bush.

"Yummy! A squirrel," shouted Fang, tearing after it.

"Fang!" cried Max as the two animals raced back toward the apartment building.

Max chased after Fang, calling, "Come back before someone sees you!"

Fang ignored him and chased the squirrel

into the backyard. Petals fell like confetti as the werepup hurtled through a large bed of flowers. Max sprinted closer and dived for the puppy, but Fang wiggled free and Max was left clutching a tuft of gray fur.

Ned is right about Fang being a handful, thought Max.

Fang wasn't going to stay a secret for long if he carried on like this.

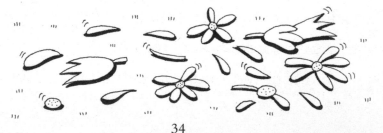

CHAPTER FIVE
ROCKET PAWS

Eventually, Max caught up with the
puppy at the base of a tree.

"Squirrel—one, Fang—zero, and serves
you right," he said, annoyed.

"I just wanted to lick it," said Fang
forlornly. "Squirrels taste yummy."

Max pulled Fang's leash out of his backpack
and buckled the collar around his neck.

"Urrrrrrrrggh!" yelled Fang. "That's
strangling me."

Max slid a finger through the collar to
check that it wasn't secured too tightly.

"It isn't!"

"It is!" said Fang angrily.

"Ned said I had to keep you a secret. Some secret! What if Mrs. Crab had seen you?"

Fang hung his head. "I'm sorry."

"That's okay."

"Will you take this off me now?"

"No way!"

"Not moving then," said Fang, plunking his fat bottom down on the ground.

"Suit yourself," said Max. "We won't go to the beach."

Max chuckled as Fang immediately leaped up, barking, "Come on, slow toes."

"Not so fast, rocket paws," said Max, holding Fang back as he rushed toward the gate at the end of the yard.

The gate led to a bush-lined alley. At first Fang walked nicely by Max's side, but the werepup was too excited to stay there for long. Soon he was darting ahead or lagging behind to sniff at interesting smells. Each time Fang pulled in a different direction, the extension leash got longer.

"It's like having a dog on a yo-yo." Max laughed.

Luckily the beach wasn't far. The moment Fang's paws stepped onto the sand, the werepup yelped with delight.

"Wait!"

Max almost had his arm pulled off as Fang galloped toward the farthest end of the beach before he stopped.

"That was great, wasn't it?" he panted.

"Yeah, great! If you like being tied to the end of a rocket," agreed Max, spitting sand out of his mouth.

He sat down, and Fang jumped in his lap

to lick his face.

"Pooh! Get off! Your breath stinks!"

"So does yours," said Fang cheerfully.

Max unclipped Fang's leash. He rummaged in his backpack for the ball and threw it across the beach.

"Fang, fetch."

"Fetch it yourself. You threw it," said Fang.

Max looked at him suspiciously.

"It's a game. I throw a ball. You go fetch it."

"I'll do the throwing," said Fang.

"That's not how the game's played."

"Then it's a stupid game," said Fang. "Let's dig a hole instead. We can both do that."

Enthusiastically, Fang began to dig, spraying sand everywhere.

"Fang, no! Stop it!" squeaked Max.

The puppy ignored him and continued digging until Max grabbed him by the collar.

"You need training," he said.

"Training?" Fang's blue eyes sparkled. "I love trains."

"Not trains! Training. Training is doing what you're told. So when I say *sit*, you sit. When I say *down*, you lie on the floor. And when I say *fetch*, you bring back the ball," said Max.

"Sounds boring," said Fang lazily.

"It isn't. It's just what you need. We'll start now. It'll be fun. I promise."

CHAPTER SIX
FULL MOON

Max spent all day with Fang. First he taught him the simple commands: sit, fetch, and down. Then he took Fang for a walk along the beach to tire him out, in the hope that Fang wouldn't spend another night howling. It was so much fun that Max stayed out longer than he meant to. Dusk was falling when he and Fang finally arrived back at Seagull Towers. Under the cover of the trees at the bottom of the yard, Max took off his backpack.

"In you go," he said.

Fang shivered. "I feel funny."

"You are funny," said Max. "Hurry up and get in."

"Look! The moon's out," Fang stared up at the darkening sky. "Ooh, it's huge! It must be . . ."

Suddenly, Fang curled back his top lip and snarled.

"Wow! What big teeth you have," joked Max.

"Grrrrrr!"

Fang began to tremble. "What's happening to me?"

Tufts of longer fur were sprouting from his ears and paws. His claws grew longer and his eyes turned bluer.

"Grrrr!"

"Oh no!" groaned Max, suddenly remembering Ned's warning. "It's a full moon. Quick! You've got to go inside."

"Nooooo," howled Fang, throwing back his head and wailing loudly.

"Yes," squeaked Max, trying to bundle Fang inside his backpack.

"Woooooo," howled Fang, digging razor-sharp claws into the ground. "Woooooooo!"

Bravely, Max shoved Fang into his rucksack, but the werepup was turning from a fat little puppy into a lean wolf cub, and he fought back furiously.

"In you go!" shouted Max.

"Woooooo!" Fang yowled.

Fear gave Max extra strength. He grabbed Fang by the scruff of the neck and rammed his backpack over the werepup's head. Fang had grown too big to fit inside, but Max held the bag in place, shouting, "Don't look at the moon!"

"Woooooo!" howled Fang, wiggling violently.

Max threw himself on top of the bag, pinning Fang to the ground. Fang kicked like an angry kangaroo, but Max held tight until gradually the werepup stopped struggling and fell silent. Was it his imagination or was Fang getting smaller again? Max continued to hold the puppy tightly, and after a very long while the puppy had shrunk enough to be squeezed back inside the backpack. Relieved, Max scooped up the bag in his arms and hurried toward the apartment building.

Max had almost reached the top of the stone steps when Fang launched a surprise attack, thrusting his head out of the top of the backpack.

"Back!" shouted Max, struggling to push the puppy's head back inside the bag.

"Woooooo!" howled Fang, gazing longingly at the moon.

Once again his top lip curled back, fur sprouted from his ears and paws, his claws grew longer, and his eyes turned bright blue.

"Grrrrrrrrrrrr," he snarled, bursting from the backpack just as Mrs. Crab came through the revolving doors.

"A dog!" she shrieked. "No dogs allowed. It's in the rules."

She lunged at Fang, who darted sideways so that Mrs. Crab almost fell down the stone steps.

"Sorry, Mrs. Crab," said Max politely. "I found this puppy in the road. He's obviously a stray, and I was taking him home when he escaped."

"Get it out of here," screeched Mrs. Crab.

Fang snarled nastily, and Mrs. Crab turned scarlet with rage. Sticking out her enormous chest, she ran, tanklike, at him.

"Got you," she shouted, grabbing him by the scruff of the neck. "Ouch! Don't you try to bite me." Mrs. Crab gave Fang a hard shake as she dragged him back up the steps.

Max raced after her.

"Thanks, Mrs. Crab. I'll take over now. The puppy's coming home with me."

"I don't think so," grunted Mrs. Crab, squeezing Fang into the revolving doors. "This is a DANGEROUS dog. First thing tomorrow I'm calling the vet to deal with it. We can't have dangerous animals running around. Now, out of my way before I have you dealt with, too."

CHAPTER SEVEN
THE ESCAPE

Max was in big trouble. There'd been a huge argument at home after he came in late, and his mom had sent him straight to his room after dinner. Not that Max had eaten much. He was too worried about Fang. Mrs. Crab had dragged Fang all the way to the boiler room, where she'd locked him inside.

Max had pleaded with her to let him take the puppy, but she'd refused and kept repeating, "That dog is dangerous. The vet can deal with it tomorrow."

Max hoped that Fang wouldn't feel too scared, shut up in the dark with a noisy old boiler. But Fang's comfort was the least of Max's problems. Max knew exactly what Mrs. Crab had meant by getting the vet to "deal" with Fang. She would have him put to sleep, like the dog that had chewed her favorite slippers.

I've got to rescue Fang, thought Max desperately.

Fang might be a bundle of mischief, but Max was already very fond of him. And what would Ned say if he knew the danger his pet was in? Miserably, Max lay on his bed staring at the ceiling. Then, suddenly, he had an idea. Grinning, Max rolled over and reached for his alarm clock.

Very early the following morning, Max arrived at Seagull Towers, leaned his bike against the stone staircase, and tiptoed in

through the revolving doors. The lobby was empty. Nervously, Max glanced around before slipping behind Mrs. Crab's counter. He went straight to her filing cabinet and rifled through the drawers. The first was jam-packed with paper clips, scissors, tape, and pens. The second contained a half-eaten package of cookies and a pile of new envelopes. But in the third Max got lucky. Right at the bottom, underneath an old newspaper, was a canister. Max opened it up and almost cheered with relief. Inside was a pile of keys, all neatly tagged and labeled.

"Boiler room," said Max, triumphantly picking out the largest key.

He held the key tightly in his hand as he hurried across the lobby and down the corridor to the boiler room. At first Max couldn't get the lock open. Frustrated, he pulled the key back out and reread the label, but it was definitely the right one. Max slowly pushed the key back in and jiggled it around. He was rewarded by a loud click, so he turned the handle and the door swung open.

"Woo, woo, woo," yapped Fang, hurling himself at Max's legs as the boy quickly shut the door behind him. "I'm sorry. What did I do? It must have been really bad for you to lock me up in here all night."

Max stared at Fang in astonishment.

"Don't you remember?"

"No," said Fang, shaking his head. "Was I really naughty?"

"I didn't lock you up. It was Mrs. Crab. You tried to bite her," said Max.

"So nothing serious," said Fang in relief.

"No, nothing serious," replied Max. "Except that now Mrs. Crab wants to get rid of you."

Fang wasn't listening. He had his nose inside an empty cookie wrapper and was gobbling up the crumbs.

"I'm starving," he said. "I found some cookies, and guess what else I found? Come over here and I'll show you."

"No," said Max firmly. "There isn't time. We've got to get out of here. This is serious. Mrs. Crab is planning to have you put down."

"Put down where?" asked Fang.

"Oh, never mind," said Max. "Quick, hop inside my backpack. I'm taking you out for the day so she can't find you."

"Yippee!" squealed Fang.

He gave the cookie wrapper one last lick and then scrambled inside Max's backpack, but when Max turned the handle of the door, it was stuck. He wiggled it and thumped it, but the door wouldn't budge. A trickle of sweat ran down Max's neck.

"Stay calm," he told himself.

In the corner of the room, Max saw a toolbox. He opened it, grabbed a hammer, and gave the door handle a hard thump. There was an ominous crack, and then the door swung open.

"Whew," Max said with a sigh, peering out into the corridor.

There was no one around. Max raced along to the lobby, replaced the boiler-room key, and then hurried outside, almost bumping into Mrs. Crab as she puffed up the stone steps.

"Good morning," he said politely.

Mrs. Crab smiled nastily.

"It will be when the vet arrives."

"You're not sick, are you?" asked Max.

The bristles on Mrs. Crab's chin wobbled furiously.

"The vet's not for me! It's for the dog that tried to savage me last night."

"Oh," said Max innocently. "Of course."

Max was eager to be as far away as possible when Mrs. Crab found the boiler room empty. He unchained his bike and pedaled off as fast as he could, with Fang hidden inside the backpack, weighing heavily on his shoulders. Max and Fang spent another great day at the beach, but this time Max was careful not to stay out too late. He sneaked Fang back into Seagull Towers long before dusk. Before he went home, Max drew all of Ned's curtains so that not one chink of moonlight could shine into the apartment. Then he made Fang promise to behave himself.

"I will," said the puppy solemnly.

Before he left, Max double-checked that he'd locked Ned's door. He was hoping to leave unseen, but unfortunately Mrs. Crab appeared in the corridor from the boiler room just as Max reached the lobby.

"You, boy!" she screeched, pointing a fat finger at him. "Plant sitter indeed! Well, I'm watching you now. I know you've taken that dog. Don't think you're going to get away with it. I'll catch you, and then you'll both be in for it."

She ran her finger across her throat,

55

leaving Max in no doubt as to what she meant.

"And I'm watching you, too," said Max under his breath.

There was something funny about Mrs. Crab. She was never around when she was needed and was always there when she wasn't. Max was sure she was up to something—if only he could find out what.

CHAPTER EIGHT

FLOOD

Arriving at Seagull Towers early the next morning, Max parked his bike and then bounced up the stone staircase. He spun through the revolving doors and found an elderly woman waiting in the lobby.

"Good morning," she said. 'I'm looking for Mrs. Crab. Have you seen her?"

"No, sorry," said Max.

Cheerfully, he hopped up the spiral staircase. If he was quick, he could smuggle Fang out of the building before Mrs. Crab appeared. But as Max entered the hallway leading to Ned's apartment, he could see bubbles seeping under the door. Max's heart raced. What had Fang done now? Max pulled the spider key out of his pocket, urging it to hurry as it leaped inside the lock. At last the front door opened, and a wall of bubbles spilled into the hallway.

"Fang!" shouted Max, pushing through them. "Urrrg, phwwt!"

The bubbles popped around him, filling his mouth with the taste of soap. His feet squelched on the slippery carpet. Carefully, Max waded along the hall and opened the kitchen door. More bubbles spilled out. Max batted them aside calling, "Fang, where are you?"

"Here, in the sink."

Max couldn't see as far as the sink. He paddled through the kitchen, banging into the table as he headed toward Fang's voice.

"Fang?"

"Here."

On the drain board, looking like a bubble sculpture, sat Fang. His ears were back and he was shaking.

"What happened?" asked Max.

Fang hung his head. "I don't know."

"You must know."

"I don't."

A funny gurgling sound made Max spin around. Not far from the sink was the washing machine, and millions of bubbles were spewing from its door. Max reached over and pressed the stop button, but the bubbles continued to churn from the machine.

"I tried that already," said Fang miserably.

"How much detergent did you use?" asked Max. "One truckload, or two?"

"I didn't," squeaked Fang. "I never touched it."

"As if!" said Max. "Washing machines don't just turn themselves on."

"It did," wailed Fang. "I was happily chewing on this stick, keeping really quiet like you told me to, when there was a green flash and the bubbles started."

"You're always just chewing on a stick," said Max.

"I'll chew the furniture if you'd prefer," said Fang.

"Wait!"

Max picked up the stick and looked at it.

There wasn't much
left of the end, but he
suddenly realized what it was.

"Oh, Fang!" Max couldn't help himself
and burst out laughing. "That's not a stick.
It's a wand."

"Yes!" Fang exclaimed. "That's what
Ned calls it! He does really clever things
with it, even though it's just his spare one."

"What, like flooding the apartment with
bubbles?"

"No!" Fang's blue eyes widened. "I
didn't . . . Did I?"

Max nodded.

Suddenly, Fang was laughing, too. He
opened his mouth and howled.

"It's not funny," Max said with a giggle.
He tried to look serious, but that made him
laugh even more.

"You're right!" howled Fang. "I almost drowned. Can you make the bubbles go away?"

"I don't know."

Max took some deep breaths and felt calmer. "I could try stopping it with the wand, but it might not work now that you've chewed off the end."

"Please try," said Fang.

"Give it here."

"Fetch!" said Fang sassily, throwing the wand to Max.

"Ha-ha!" said Max, reaching out and catching the wand just as the kitchen door opened. He stared in horror.

"Er, hello, Mrs. Crab. How did you get in?"

"The door was open," snapped Mrs. Crab. "Why all the noise, and WHO made all this mess?"

"Me," said Max. "I'm doing some laundry."

"Laundry?!" screeched Mrs. Crab.

Her face was redder than a traffic light and the bristles on her chin stuck out like daggers.

"NEVER, in forty years as a caretaker, has anyone flooded one of my apartments, until now."

"It's Ned's apartment, not yours!" growled Fang.

Mrs. Crab spun around, confused. Max, finger to his lips, shook his head warningly at Fang. Fang's blue eyes widened. Then he quickly shut his mouth.

"Ha!" Luckily, Mrs. Crab was too angry to realize it was Fang who had spoken. "I knew I'd catch you in the end. It's that dangerous dog. I'm calling the vet to deal with it right now."

Max wasn't sure what happened next. One moment he was holding Ned's wand in front of him, the next it was pointing straight at Mrs. Crab's bristly chin. There was a loud crack, a strange hissing noise, and then a stream of orange stars shot from the wand and whizzed around the kitchen. Max coughed. A lone star spluttered from

the tip of the wand and fizzled away. Behind him the washing machine belched loudly. Max spun around, punching the air with delight when he saw that it had finally turned itself off.

"I did it. I stopped the washing machine!" he cried, waving Ned's wand.

There was no reply. The kitchen was empty.

"Fang?" Max waded over to the sink, but Fang had gone. So had Mrs. Crab, and a cold panic set in Max's stomach. Mrs. Crab had taken Fang away. Something was thumping. It was louder than an army of marching giants. Max stared around the room before realizing that the noise was coming from his own heart. Suddenly he felt breathless, and that made him angry. How dare Mrs. Crab take Fang away! He would follow her and demand she give him back. As Max splashed to the door, a voice called down the hall . . .

"Hello!"

CHAPTER NINE
MRS. CRAB

"Is Mrs. Crab here? I heard her voice."

The elderly woman who had been waiting at Mrs. Crab's desk in the lobby earlier stuck her head around the front door. Max was so relieved to see her that he laughed. For one awful moment he'd thought that Ned had come home early.

"What happened?" asked the woman kindly. "Did the washing machine burst a pipe?"

"Several," said Max, his brain whirring so fast he thought that it might burst, too.

"Mrs. Crab's gone. Didn't she pass you?"

"No, thank goodness." The woman grinned. "She's not the best person to meet in a narrow hallway."

"Er, no. Exactly," said Max. "Don't come any farther. The floor's really slippery."

Max stood in the kitchen doorway, blocking the woman's view. His heart was thumping again. He'd just noticed a large rock-shaped creature half submerged in bubbles. It looked very out of place in Ned's kitchen. A horrible thought crossed Max's mind. No, that was ridiculous. It couldn't be, could it? Furtively, Max glanced at the creature again and almost groaned out loud. This was turning into a nightmare! Max started to laugh. He always laughed when he was in trouble, even though this definitely wasn't a laughing matter.

"I need a bucket," he said, forcing himself

to be serious. "Can you lend me one?"

"Of course I can!" said the woman. "Back in a second."

Max didn't really need a bucket. He just needed the woman out of the way. When she'd left, Max shut the front door and chained it. Reluctantly, he returned to the kitchen. The creature hadn't moved. Max bent down for a closer look at the large crab sitting on Ned's kitchen floor. It had six jointed legs, a pair of pincers, two beady black eyes, and, unusually for a crab, bristles. Max prodded it with Ned's wand, and the crab angrily waved a claw.

"Mrs. Crab!" Max collapsed with laughter. "Mrs. Crab's turned into a crab! But how?"

"You did it." Fang splashed through the kitchen door, and Max hugged him with relief.

"Where've you been? You gave me such a fright when you disappeared."

"You said I was a secret, so I hid."

"Oh, Fang!" Max hugged the werepup again. "It's too late. Mrs. Crab saw you."

"I know. So you turned her into a crab," said Fang, chuckling.

"I didn't mean to!" Guiltily, Max stared at the wand. "Oh, bat poo!"

"But that's good! Now she can't send for the vet. Thank you, Max. You're the best pet sitter ever."

Fang threw himself on Max, causing a mini tidal wave that sent the crab scuttling away.

"Quick," said Max, splashing after her. "Shut the door before she escapes."

Fang nosed the door shut.

"We'll have to put her somewhere safe. I know! The bathtub," said Max.

He put Ned's wand on the table, but as he drew closer to Mrs. Crab, she snapped her enormous claws at him.

"Pinch me and I'll put you on the grill," Max threatened.

Mrs. Crab's shell turned scarlet. She banged a claw on the ground, splattering Max with bubbles, but she didn't pinch him when he lifted her up. She weighed a ton, and Max crossed the kitchen groaning.

"Out of the way, Fang."

Max knew nothing about crabs besides the fact that they were sea creatures. He went to

71

the bathroom, put a few inches of cold water into the bathtub, and threw in Ned's rubber ducky for company. Then, shutting the bathroom door firmly behind him, he

went to answer a knock at the front door.

It was the woman, and she had two buckets and a sponge.

"Thanks," said Max.

"Need any help?" she asked.

"No, thanks."

'Well, if you're sure." The woman sounded disappointed. "If you change your mind, I'm at number sixteen."

"Thanks," said Max. "And thanks for the buckets."

When the woman had gone, Max bolted the front door. Fang was sitting on the kitchen table chewing Ned's wand. Max snatched it away.

"Don't chew that!" he scolded.

"I'm a puppy. It's my job to chew things," said Fang.

"I'm the pet sitter. It's my job to stop you," said Max, examining the wand. The end was soggy and badly chewed. Experimentally, Max waved it around. Did he dare use it to turn Mrs. Crab back into herself? Perhaps he should try using it for something else first. Max decided to try cleaning up the kitchen.

"Stand back," he told Fang.

Nervously, Max waved the wand over a small patch of floor.

"Wand, dry. Please."

73

A flash of red light burst from the wand, instantly melting the bubbles. A spiral of steam curled upward as the floor dried.

"Go, Max!" cheered Fang.

"Cool!" exclaimed Max, and feeling braver, he waved the wand around again.

"Wand, dry. Please," he repeated.

Another flash of red. Hiss, pop, crack. The bubbles burst, sounding like a giant bowl of Rice Krispies. Steam rose from the floor, and soon the kitchen was hotter than a jungle.

"Whew!" said Max, opening the window. "That didn't take long."

With the kitchen dry, Max started on the hallway. "Wand, dry," he said, more boldly this time.

There was a flash of red, lots of steam, and a bitter smell.

"Pooh!" said Max, and then, realizing he'd set fire to the carpet, he waved the

wand again. "Wand, fire out."

The flames spluttered and went out, leaving a small charred patch.

"Cool!" Fang said with a sigh. "Shame about the carpet, though."

"Silly me!" agreed Max. "'Cause you'd never make a mess, would you?!"

Chapter Ten
Fang Runs Off

Max was in a dilemma. Deep down he knew he must use Ned's wand to turn Mrs. Crab back into her human self. Crabby as she was (Max snickered at the bad joke), it wasn't right to leave her in that state. But Fang was dead set against the idea.

"Don't do it," he wailed dramatically. "She's going to have me dealt with, and what then? Ned would never forgive you."

"But I can't leave her as she is," said Max. "What if she has a family who'll miss her? We'll just have to be more careful. Especially you! No more howling and no more chewing Ned's wand."

Before Max changed Mrs. Crab back, he made Fang hide in Ned's bedroom closet.

"What if she comes looking for me?" he asked.

"She won't," said Max firmly. "I'll have Ned's wand, remember. If she tries anything funny, I'll turn her back into a crab."

"Cool," said Fang. "I hope she does."

"Shh," said Max as he closed the closet door.

Slowly he went into the bathroom.

"Ugh!" he exclaimed. "She must be hungry!"

Mrs. Crab was eating Ned's rubber ducky; only its plastic beak remained. Max waved the wand, and then, pointing it at the bathtub, he said clearly, "Wand, undo."

There was a loud crack. Black smoke

shot from the end of the wand, smothering everything. Max held his breath, wondering if his spell had worked. Then suddenly the air cleared and Max bit his tongue, trying not to laugh. There, in a bathtub full of cold water, sat Mrs. Crab. Her clothes were soaking and she had a plastic duck's beak stuck on her nose.

Max passed her one of Ned's towels,

saying, "Hello, Mrs. Crab. Did you enjoy your bath?"

Mrs. Crab pulled the duck beak from her nose. She shook her head a few times and then slowly stood up. Water gushed from her clothes like a waterfall.

"I'm not sure how I got here, but this I do know," she growled. "I'm going to catch that dog if it's the last thing I do."

Mrs. Crab climbed out of the bathtub and marched out of the bathroom.

Max guessed that Mrs. Crab wouldn't go back to work right away, and he was right. There was no sign of her when he smuggled Fang out of the building for their daily outing. All this sneaking in and out was beginning to get to Max, and he wished there was some way of making Mrs. Crab leave him and Fang alone.

★ ★ ★

After a fun day at the beach, Max was starving and looking forward to going home for dinner. He let Fang walk to the top of Seagull Tower's driveway before stopping to hide him inside his backpack.

"In you go, fatty," he teased.

Fang stood stiller than a statue. Then suddenly he took off toward the building.

"Fang!" shouted Max. "Fang, come back. I was just kidding."

Fang ignored him. He raced up the stone steps and through the revolving doors. Max followed, accidentally whirling around twice before he managed to jump out. He was in time to see Fang speed off down the hallway toward the boiler room.

"Fang," hissed Max, half angry, half scared. What was the werepup up to? He was behaving as if he wanted to get caught. When Max finally caught up with Fang, he was throwing himself at the boiler-room door. Max grabbed him by the collar and hauled him backward. Fang stuck his claws in the carpet and refused to move.

"Someone's in there," he yapped. "Can't you hear them shouting for help?"

Max stared suspiciously at Fang, but the werepup was serious. Then he heard it, too. Inside the boiler room someone was wailing like a baby.

"I wonder who Mrs. Crab's locked in there this time," said Max angrily. "Hello?" He banged on the door with his fist. "Are you all right?"

There was no reply, but when Max pressed his ear to the door, he heard a groan. Then he noticed that the key was

in the lock. He turned it, but nothing happened. Then he wiggled the key this way and that, but the lock was jammed. He tried to force the door open. He banged and banged, but it wouldn't budge.

"Should I get Ned's wand?" offered Fang.

"No need."

Suddenly, remembering a police raid in a movie he'd watched, Max aimed a karate-style kick at the lock. The door shuddered. Max kicked again, and this time the lock broke and the door flew open.

"Wow!" said Fang, staring at the damage. "How cool was that?"

"As cool as a hippo on ice skates," said Max. "But not as careful!"

CHAPTER ELEVEN
THE DEAL

Lying on the boiler-room floor, with a folding chair wedged on top of her, was Mrs. Crab. She looked so funny that Max had a tough job not laughing out loud. She was moaning, but she wasn't hurt and recovered

immediately when Max helped her up.

"The lock's broken," she grumbled. "I couldn't get out. I was trying to unscrew the door hinges when I fell off the chair. I shouted for help, but nobody came. I've been stuck in here all day."

"That happened to me!" said Fang.

Max glared at him, wishing Fang had had the sense to hide, but it was too late. Mrs. Crab spun around. Her eyes narrowed.

"It's that dog!" she exclaimed. Again she didn't realize that it was Fang who'd spoken —she was too excited at having caught Max. "And this time I'm calling the vet."

Mrs. Crab pushed her way past Max.

"Wait," he called. "It was Fang who heard you shouting. He led me to you."

"And?" said Mrs. Crab nastily.

"And . . ."

Suddenly, Max noticed a messy pile of
newspapers next to the boiler. He
stepped closer and pushed them
aside. Underneath was a kettle,
a mug, a jar of coffee, and
several packages of cookies.

"That's why no one can ever find you!
You've been skipping work, hiding in here
drinking coffee and stuffing yourself with
cookies."

The bristles on Mrs. Crab's chin trembled,
and Max could see she that was scared.

"You have, haven't you?" He grinned.
"Well, here's the deal: if you promise not to
call the vet and you let Fang stay here at
Seagull Towers, then I won't tell anyone
that you've been bunking. After all, you
wouldn't want to lose your job, would you?"

For once, Mrs. Crab was speechless.

★ ★ ★

The following day, Max and Fang sat on the steps that led up to Seagull Towers waiting for Ned to come home.

"Ooooh!" squealed Fang.

"What?" asked Max. "Can you see Ned?"

"No." Fang dived into the bushes. "I need to go."

"Again? You've just been."

"I can't help it," said Fang, his black nose just visible through the branches. "I always go when I'm excited."

"Hurry up," said Max. "Ned's coming up the driveway right now."

"Oooooh!" Fang ran back and almost knocked Max over.

"Whoa!" Max grabbed him by the collar. "Slow down. You can't go meet Ned like that. He'll think you're a mobile tree."

Hurriedly, Max picked leaves and twigs from Fang's coat. The werepup strained on his collar, growling like an engine. When Max finally let him go, he raced toward Ned, who was staggering up the driveway with two suitcases and a large package.

"Hello, hello, hello," Fang barked. "I've missed you soooooo much."

"And I've missed you, too," said Ned, dumping the bags and scooping Fang up in his arms. "Have you been good or were you a wicked little werepup?"

"Fang's been very good," said Max. "We went for walks, we played on the beach, and"—Max winked at Fang—"we even did some crabbing."

"So nothing exciting," said Ned cheerfully. "Never mind—Daddy's home now, and spider's teeth, he going to liven this place up! Down with silly rules! Look what my sister gave me as a thank you for helping her out with the camp."

Ned pulled the paper away from the mysterious package to reveal a shiny new skateboard.

"Cool!" said Fang. "Can I have a try?"

"Visitors first," said Ned, holding it out to Max.

"Thanks," said Max, longing to try the skateboard but thinking he'd broken enough rules already, "but I can't stay. I've got another pet to look after now. Take care, Fang! You, too, Ned!"

Me and Fang!

About the Author

Julie Sykes has had more than thirty books published, including several about her creation Little Tiger. Among her other titles are *That Pesky Dragon*, *Dora's Eggs*, and *Hurry, Santa!* Her books *I Don't Want to Go to Bed!* and *I Don't Want to Have a Bath!* won the Nottingham Children's Book Award. Julie has three children and lives in Hampshire, England.

About the Illustrator

Nathan Reed has illustrated children's stories for Puffin, HarperCollins, and Campbell Books. He also illustrated one of the most popular titles in Kingfisher's I Am Reading series, *Hocus Pocus Hound*. Nathan lives in London, England.

The Pet Sitter by Julie Sykes
illustrated by Nathan Reed

Keep up with Max, the pintsize hero, as he pet-sits unusual animals.

Now available:

TIGER TAMING ISBN: 978-0-7534-6271-3 $5.99 ($6.99 CAN)
A witch's cat proves to be a handful—talking back and getting kidnapped.

DIXIE IN DANGER ISBN: 978-0-7534-6217-1 $5.99 ($6.99 CAN)
Caring for a sleepy dormouse couldn't be easier. But then again . . .

PARROT PANDEMONIUM ISBN: 978-0-7534-6219-5 $5.99 ($7.75 CAN)
Casting out to sea with Squawk the parrot is not Max's idea of fun.

BEWARE THE WEREPUP ISBN: 978-0-7534-6218-8 $5.99 ($7.75 CAN)
Max's main priority is to give Fang his walks and avoid full moons.

OTHER BOOKS YOU WILL ENJOY:
QUENTIN QUIRK'S MAGIC WORKS by Matt Kain
illustrated by Jim Field

Introducing Jez and Charlie, two chaotic but likable
heroes of a brand-new magic-themed series.

ATTACK OF THE BUTT-BITING SHARKS
ISBN: 978-0-7534-6294-2 $5.99 ($7.75 CAN)

THE PURPLE SLUGGY WORRY WARTS
ISBN: 978-0-7534-6295-9 $5.99 ($7.75 CAN)

KINGFISHER
NEW YORK
www.kingfisherpublications.com

Available at bookstores nationwide